Table of contents

Date with Lois

After driving with Lois to Tahoe Ridge Vineyards and Winery, about an hour south of Reno, we taste a few vintages and buy a 2020 Chardonnay to share on the covered porch. After a few samplings of wine I have a persistent buzz going on. So I suggest a walk through the vineyard would be just the ticket to clear my head a little.

Soon, we embrace and the clover growing between the vines provides an invitingly soft cushion for us to sink onto, maintaining our embrace and continuing the duel with our tongues.

Lois is whimpering, but I reassure her that she is the most desirable woman on the planet. I pick up the subtle aroma of her arousal and decide to carry this interlude further. The moment is ripe and time hangs in the balance as we stare into each other's eyes, unable to break our gaze, but fully aware of the physiology, and scents, and subtle welcoming movements that are prelude to an even more joyous union. Divesting Lois of her shorts, panties and bra, I concentrate on delivering seductive licks along her slit, playful flicks against her clit, and serious jabs that invade the steamy grotto that opens wider with every swipe of my tongue. Her inner lips are turning redder as they become engorged with blood, wetter as her body produces the secretions of love, and odiferous with the pheromones of desire. She moans and thrashes as I celebrate the wondrous creation that is Lois and know that in this moment, she loves being a woman.

There is no greater (well, almost) happiness than to bring a woman to a shattering orgasm. I am supremely happy, full of my maleness and charged with testosterone. My face is a mess, but it is from Lois's body; the divine essence of a goddess, and I have been baptized into a great mystery.

After cuddling together for the long moments it takes to restore reasonable respiration, we slowly sit up together. Lois's gaze takes me in, tears glistening in her eyes. She cannot fail to see that my cock is as rigid as rebar, super hard and straining through the opening of my unzipped pants. Murmuring seductively, she says, "It's your turn now," as she opens my pants a bit wider and brings the full length into view. It is beautifully shaped, nothing grotesque or beyond what she can handle. In anticipation, she starts to salivate and asks, "Can I suck it?"

“Go for it,” I answer, laughing because she is so polite to ask after what we have just shared. Within seconds she has twisted around to take me into her mouth, after first lapping it like a kitten after milk.

Lois starts slowly at the head of my savory appendage, swirling her tongue around it as she tightens her lips around the ring of the helmet. It feels every bit as good as it looked and she hears my moan and feels me push to get deeper into her mouth. She teases at first, sucking only the head of my cock and licking the sides of the shaft. But soon she is taking it fully into her mouth, pressing it toward the back of her throat. It makes her gag a little when she tries to deep throat me, but she gets past the gagging and slips the full length into her throat. Mmm, I’m sliding in deep and she manages to swallow and hold me for a few seconds before coming up for air. She does it again and it goes down easier this time.

She swallows it several more times and that is all I can take; I tell her that I’m going to cum and she pops it from her lips.

“Cum in my mouth,” Lois says with a tone of excitement. She opens her mouth wide and allows me to jerk off until my hot, white jism spurts from my cock and lands on her tongue. Two, three, four squirts and I’m completely coating her tongue. I can tell that she loves it as she grabs my cock from my hand and shoves it back into her mouth, sucking and swallowing like the hot little slut that she has become at this moment.

I am spent for the moment and can only lie there in a euphoric haze as Lois finish cleaning me with her mouth and tongue. We lock eyes again, this time not in anticipation but in utter satisfaction and wonder. We both start laughing. It’s a joyful laugh, a laugh of fulfillment and completion ... for the moment ... though we both know with certainty that this is nowhere near finished ... perhaps never.

Cock Sucking

Ellie calls her friend Paige in accounting. “Want to go get lunch?”

“Oh, you know what, I can’t,” Paige says. “I’m working on this special project.”

“For work? We’re supposed to have the day off.”

“Not work work,” Paige says. “It’s ... it’s kinda hard to explain.”

“I’ve got time,” Ellie says. “Maybe I can help.”

Paige laughs.

“What’s so funny?” Ellie asks.

“Oh, nothing. It’s just sort of personal. An inside joke.”

“Tell.”

“I’d be too embarrassed.”

“Come on. We’ve known each other since we were ten. We wet our pants together in Girl Scouts. What could be more embarrassing than that?”

“Geeze—I’d forgotten about that. That was embarrassing.”

“So what’s this special project?”

“Okay, well ... it’s Mike and I’s anniversary in two weeks. A year since we first met.”

“That’s right—the blackjack thing the church put on.”

“Right. Vegas Night. I was one of the dealers, and he kept losing and losing and losing. Making one wild bet after another. Asking for an extra card even when he had blackjack. He was so impossible.”

“But it was for a good cause,” Ellie reminds Paige. “The victims of ... what was it?”

“I think I was the cause,” Paige says. “Anyway, he really made me laugh. ‘Hit me hit me hit me,’ he kept saying. ‘Oh, yeah, hit me again.’ ”

“Naughty boy,” Ellie says. “Sounds like he was after a good hard spanking.”

“Ha ha. Anyway, finally he ran out of tickets. And he asked me if he could have one back, so he could enter the end of the evening raffle.”

“What was the prize?”

“A trip to Vegas. Fitting, huh?”

“Did you give him back his ticket?”

“I did. I shouldn’t have, but he was so irresistible. He said if he won he’d take me to Vegas with him.”

“Did he win?”

Paige laughs. “No. But he took me to Vegas anyway.”

“I didn’t know that part of the story,” Ellie admits. “Wow, Vegas. Did he win there?”

“Um,” Paige says.

“What?”

“We never really left the hotel room. It was sort of like a honeymoon. Except without the marriage part.”

“Wow.”

“I know.”

“Mike is a sweetie. You should marry him. Go to Vegas on a real honeymoon.”

“He keeps asking me. He’s very persistent.”

“Don’t you want to marry him?”

“I do. Mostly. But I don’t want to rush into it. I don’t want one of those starter marriages.”

“Makes sense.”

“But if he asks me on our one-year anniversary, I might say yes.”

“Oh, Paige.”

“I know.”

“I don’t want to go to Vegas on the honeymoon, though. Been there, done that.”

“Where do you want to go?”

“I don’t know. A South Sea Island? Someplace with warm breezes and swaying palm trees, waterfalls and a midnight blue lagoon.”

“Sounds perfect,” Ellie says. “Marry me! Take me there!”

“Ha ha.”

“So what’s the special project?”

“Oh, right. It’s going to sound stupid.”

“Try me.”

“It’s a deck of cards.”

“Ah. In honor of your Vegas night. Fitting.”

“Right. It’s sort of a gag gift.”

“You mean like a marked deck or something?”

“Or something. I was just being cute.”

“So what’s special about it? Come on, spit it out!”

“Okay. Okay. You know how playing cards have pictures on them?”

“Sure. The king, the queen. The jacks and jokers.”

“No, you’re thinking of face cards. I mean on the backs.”

“Oh, right. Face cards.”

“Well there’s this Internet place that lets you pick your own picture, then they print up the deck.”

“Neat. So which picture did you pick? One of you and him, I suppose.”

“Well, I have one in mind, but it’s...”

“It’s what.”

“It’s sort of naughty.”

“How naughty?

“Very naughty.”

“Oh my! Are you like naked or something?”

“I’m a little embarrassed to say.”

“You have to tell me. We’ve come this far.”

“The idea is that these cards are sort of like coupons.”

“Coupons?”

“Yeah, like he can redeem them one at a time for certain ... favors.”

“Sounds interesting. But you haven’t told me what’s on the cards.”

“It’s a picture of us, of me, really, with Mike’s penis in my mouth.”

“Oh, Paige.”

“I know.”

“So you’re giving him a blow job?”

“I don’t like to call it that.”

“What do you call it?”

“A cock sucking.”

“Tom always calls it a blow job. Actually he calls it a bee-jay. He says, ‘Hey, babe, how ‘bout a little bee-jay.’ Or sometimes he says, ‘How ‘bout a little bee-jay action.’ ”

The line is quiet for a few seconds, then Ellie says, “So he can give you one of these cards in exchange for a free blow job. I mean cock-sucking.”

“Right.”

“How many cards are there?”

“Fifty-five. I guess there’s the full deck, plus three jokers. But that works out. I figure one for each week, one for his birthday, one for our ‘anniversary,’ and one ‘floater.’ ”

“That’s funny,” Ellie says. “Sound a little like it’s underwater—this ‘floater’ bee-jay. Have you ever done it underwater?”

“In the shower sometimes. That’s kind of fun—unless the hot water runs out.”

“Tom likes it in the shower. But a real waterfall might be better. Like on your tropical island.”

“Yes, an island would be nice. A waterfall would be nice.”

“So you have fifty-five different pictures of you giving him head. How did you get them?”

“No, there aren’t that many. And I’m just using the one. I think that’s all that’s allowed. In the one I’m thinking of, I’m looking up at him, and I think my eyes look really pretty, in a lewd but loving sort of way.”

“Mmm,” Ellie says. “You’ll have to show me this lewd but loving look sometime. Maybe you can teach it to me.”

“Ha ha.”

“So Mike took this picture?”

“Who else would have taken it?”

“I don’t know. I was just asking. How far in is he? How much of him can you see?”

“Ellie, you’re making me nervous with these questions.”

“I just want to know. It sounds really hot.”

“He was in pretty far but not all the way.”

“Can you get him all the way in?”

“Ellie!”

“Okay, I was just asking. I have trouble getting more than half of Tom in my mouth. But he likes it better when I nibble him from the side anyway. Like an ear of corn. When I slide my whole mouth back and forth.”

“Mike likes that too. He likes everything. That’s why I thought this would be such a good gift.”

“Do you take his balls, too? Do you like his balls in your mouth?”

“Ellie.”

“Can you see his balls in the picture?”

“Ellie.”

“Okay. Sorry. Just one more question. When he comes in your mouth, do you swallow? Do you like the way he tastes?"

"That's two questions."

"Sorry."

"One time I did," Paige says.

"One time you swallowed?"

"No, one time I took his balls in my mouth. We were at this hotel, and in the morning he took the first shower, and when he came into the room I was lying on the bed with my head over the edge, and he sort of swayed up to me and put his legs around my face. His balls were right in my face, all clean and wooly, so naturally I started licking, and eventually I sort of sucked his balls, one of them anyway, into my mouth. It felt sort of neat, unlike anything I'd had in my mouth before, and my nose was right in his—in his crease."

"In his asshole?"

"Almost in his asshole, and I thought, this is so hot, and I thought about licking him there."

"Wow, that is hot. Did you do it?"

"No, I chickened out. I sort of slid forward just a little, or maybe it's backward, so I could get his cock in my mouth. I had to pull it down, it was so big and stiff, and he helped by leaning forward, bracing himself with his hand on the bed, I guess, and licking my belly button."

"Ooh. Do you like getting your belly button licked?

"Sometimes. Sometimes it tickles too much."

"I'll have to remember that."

"You knew that, Ellie! From Girl Scouts, remember?"

"Oh, yeah, that's right. Now I remember. We tickled each other until we peed."

"You peed first. I just did it because..."

"Because what?" Ellie asks.

"Because I don't know. I didn't want you to feel lonely. Left out."

"Did you pee when Mike tickled your belly button?"

"No, he was only licking me there for a minute. Then he sort of jerked back and lifted me up. He was holding me by my hips with my legs over his shoulders. He was licking my middle and I was upside down, still sucking him. It was really exciting. He pushed his tongue deep deep in me, and I just kept sucking. And I could feel his chin on my mound, pressing me hard, and I used my hand on him, my hand and my mouth, and part of me wondered if he’ d drop me when he came.”

“Did he?”

“He came, but he didn’ t drop me. Mike is so strong! My big strong man. His legs might have buckled a bit, but he sort of swiveled around and sat back and then lay back on the bed. My mouth was full of his cum and I was riding him, riding his face and his chin, like he was a big stallion with his cock fucking my cunt, only it was his tongue fucking my cunt, and I rode and I rode.”

“Did you come?”

“Oh, God, yes. I came and came. When I finally stopped coming, his face was drenched with my juice.”

“Did you swallow his stuff?”

“Oh, Lordy, I don’ t remember. Probably. Or maybe it just seeped out.”

“That’ s the way it is with me and Tom. Sometimes I swallow, sometimes I don’ t. He doesn’ t seem to mind either way. Sometimes it’ s hard to get it down. Hard to get it all spit out, too. The easiest thing is to just keep sucking him until it sort of goes away. Either gets swallowed or leaks out. Of course, by then he’ s hard again, and it starts all over again.”

“Mm. Sounds like you guys do this a real lot.”

“He really likes it. I like it, too.”

“Maybe you should give Tom a deck of cards.”

“Maybe, except I don’ t have a picture.”

“How often do you do it?”

“Suck Tom’ s cock?”

“Yeah.”

“Maybe two or three times a week.”

“So you’ d probably need to give him two decks.”

“Right.”

"Since I only get to see Mike on weekends, one deck is probably enough for us, don't you think?"

"I guess. But look, do you trust this Internet place? What if they, like, use the picture?"

"I can't print the cards myself," Paige says. "I guess I have to trust them. Sort of like a doctor, you know? Or a tattoo artist. If you get a really intimate tattoo."

"Do you have a really intimate tattoo?"

"No. But it would be sort of the same thing, wouldn't it?"

"Yeah, but the tattoo artist, or the doctor, doesn't have a picture of your—of your whatever. I mean if he's a doctor, maybe he has an x-ray, but not a real picture."

"True."

"So this place lets you send in X-rated stuff?"

"I think so. Ellie, you're making me nervous again. I thought this would be such a neat idea."

"It is a neat idea. I think you should do it."

"You do?"

"But what if Mike doesn't ask you to marry him? What if he just takes his fifty-five free blow jobs, I mean cocksuckings, and then...?"

"Then what?"

"Then nothing."

The line is silent for a while.

"Okay, Ellie, you've talked me out of it. Bad idea. Let's go to lunch."

"I don't think I can right now," Ellie says. "There's this conference call starts at one."

"Oh. I guess I blabbered too long, huh?"

"But look," Ellie says, "this weekend, why don't you and Mike come over? Maybe we can play some cards."

My First Lesbian Experience

My first ever lesbian lover now fucks me

She and my mandawg lover had just gone over me fine tooth and comb, and I had multiple gushing orgasms for the first time in my life from the tonguing and licking over all my body, and my second female to female kissing experience, OMG did they work me over!

Now it was time She fucked me! Dawg just began to suck me small tiny titties and go at my hardened nipples biting and sucking them up from my tit flesh making me scream and cry out as he did this my passion already so inflamed every touch of my body sent me into orbit with pleasure.

I guess he was doing this to distract me from her having now discarded the towel on the little bed and she got up and left again.

Then again as he had stopped his mouth and tongues working over of both my tits and nipples, I coming down from yet another almost blacking out orgasm I heard her at that door and unbolting it again from the outside, then she brought her naked hind end in through the door first, there were straps around her thighs two sets really one lower down and the other right up under her beautiful full womanly rounded out ass, and then a strap was above all that around her waist.

As I’ ve said before I just a naÃ¯ve country girl, and I’ ve never seen any of this ever in my life I had absolutely no idea what she had or what it was all about at all as she being face to the door closed and locked it up again, and had a large towel in her one hand and immediately threw it around herself as it feel to her knees looking at her back.

Then she turned and I gasped out loud as I could, and I saw that towel tented way out from between her legs a thick, really thick, bulge was under that towel, what it was and what it looked like as yet I had no clue of.

But as she walked towards me tied up on the altar like I was and him right beside me now leaning over and kissing me on the lips and in another hot kissing session of our own, and rose up and said; Jackie your about to get fucked by another woman!

My eyes were wide open seeing her coming towards me, that huge bulge under that towel swinging and dancing about under it, as she said to me; I am going to fuck you like you have never ever been fucked sweetie pie!

Whatever it was under there was fucking HUGE and I mean HUGE!

As she came over to the altar my being so tied up as I was both legs and arms above me and spread to the corners of both the top and bottom my legs widely spread apart and tied in the air as they were, and I wide open for whatever she wanted to fuck me with.

And now right there in front of me standing right at my head she lowered a hand down and grasp what was under that towel and It was so thick her hand could not even go around it, which made me scream out, and my eyes shot wide open in horror knowing whatever it was she was going to fuck me with it!

I began screaming out that’ s to big for me, that’ s to big for me Oh please don’ t even try, it will split me apart and tear me wide open!

Oh yeah she cried out and said; That’ s how I love them to act when I fuck another woman.

Even he had his eyes wide open in such disbelief that she had this huge ass thing under that towel to fuck me with it.

He himself said; (calling her by her name)you can’ t use that! It will tear her pussy apart!

Jackie has hard enough time even taking me (calling her name) damn what made you think she could take such a damn monster as that?

Oh she’ ll take it alright Dawg oh hell yeah she’ ll take it, she sure may come unglued, but she’ ll take it. She Said.

I’ ll be as gentle, and easy as I can with it sweetie pie, and we’ re going to get that little belly of yours busted wide open with it.

After standing right there doing that torture to me about it she released it walked over to her corner cabinets and reached in grabbed a wedge like pillow looking thing, then coming back over that huge thing swinging about like pendulum under the towel and stopped again right at my head.

And tossed him the pillow and told him put it right up under her neck and that will raise her head up as he slid it under my head and neck, my head rose up to where I could fully see right down to my red haired mound all matted up from my orgasms and her mouth consuming some of it.

Ahhhh Yeah she said; Just exactly right my sweetie pie I want to see and feel it as it happens! Damn I love when they have to watch it, and feel it working into their tight little pussies!

I was just screaming out over and over again; Oh please don’t do it! Oh please don’t do it!

Screaming at him to help me, and to stop her from doing it!

He told me there was nothing he could do to stop her, if he even tried, she would horrendously punish us both.

She said; That’s exactly right my little sweetie pie if he tries to stop me, I will summoned up a Demon Beast to come fuck you!

Not from that clan that the visiting entity was from No. But sweetie pie there are others I can summon up to come here.

Once I fill your little belly and pussy up with huge dick you will see why I gave you the injections to open your pussy up as it is now and ready to take your first ever really huge cock! Dawgs got a pretty good sized one, but no man I know of sweetie pie has anything like what’s under this towel!

And sweetie pie I’ll give you just a tiny little hint before I go down and drop the towel for all to see.

With that said she raised on leg up on the altar the towel coming over my head and what I saw scared me to DEATH!

I screamed out Oh please no nothing like that, Oh please no, I don’t want one like that.

Then as I lay there panting and screaming out not one like that my whole body shuddered in my bondage as I was the horrible fear of what she was about to fuck me had me scared to death. She just pulled her hiked leg off the bed and stood there

He said what to hell is it? And as I was about to tell him she reached down and grabbed my mouth closing it shut with her hand over it.

She just looked at me and said; Oh no Sweetie Pie this only our little secret at the moment. You say one word to him about it and I’ll get a shot and inject your little ass so you’ll be so far gone you can’t talk!

I now knew the cruelty of which she could bestow upon someone, and the outright evil hideous way she could it.

She was going to outright fuck me with something I’d long forgotten about well at least till recently when all of it surfaced up with all this that is.

Even now I' m sitting here writing this and to damn terrified even now to fully disclose what was under that towel.

It will soon be fully known.

It was horrendously shaped and just a mere thought of it even now as I write this scares me.

I lay there saying nothing to him at all for fear and knowing she would go get a shot and give it to me and goodness only knows what it would have done and made me do.

But I was shaking like a leaf in a hurricane, my eyes shot wide open in the horrific thing I' d seen under that towel, even now I wonder just where to hell she even found something like that especially back then, when nothing was available like sex toys now are!

As she just turned and walked away going back over to that cabinet on the floor reached into it and pulled something out and turned to come over to us.

There in her hands was what looked like some canteen looking thing which in fact it was just that but it was different in that right in the lid of it was a small nipple coming up out of it and it had a battery that somehow it looked like the bag was made by her that had both together in it.

My eyes shot even wider open at seeing her bringing this thing over as she just walked to the foot of the altar and sat it down right there close to my where my ass was on it and there was a long clear hose plugged into that nipple as she uncoiled the long hose and left it dangling off the altar onto the floor.

He asked her; (calling her by name)Just what the fuck is that for?

She told him he' d know soon enough and that I sure as hell would after she got me full of that huge cock and fucked good with it!

He asked her what the fuck do you have in that canteen and she said; I will not say for now until I am ready to use it.

He was absolutely right you do not cross a bitch like this she would probably kill you and I felt she was about to do just that when she tried to fuck me with that horrific thing under that towel.

Now it made full sense to me why she had injected my ass with those shots was to get me in somewhat a condition to be anywhere near what that huge horrendous thing was going to do to my pussy!

With now having sat that thing on the altar she went right up between my spread open legs and said; Time to unveil my special toy to fuck her with.

Absolutely now in some crazed evil fashion she was singing out Ta Dun Dunn Dunn and then pulled the towel free.

And there for us all to see was a horrendous huge cock that looked just exactly like a DOG COCK!

In perfect exact replica of what a real one looked like except way way bigger and a long tapered tip on the end of it almost a off white color it was going back to where the head was that was flared out at the joining of where the tip tapered down to and it was all a hot red color deep blue veins showing up all along it

The tip of it the size of a round magic marker and about as long, with a clearly defined and noticeable hole in very end, at the head of it was a long taper to the tip, and a rough rib like swell all around the start of the shaft much in way like an uncircumcised cock flare, on a mans cock then it was rough just behind that where it joined the huge thick shaft slick as it could be then bright and shiny but dark hot red colored all the way back on the rest of it.

Then it final- ed with a huge round knot at near the base the size of a large orange and still several inches more of cock shaft where it was held into the strap on at. And there coming from up under where it held tight and firmly in the strap on that ran underneath it all was a long neck of a hose connector which now she had reached and grabbed the hose and snuggly pushed it onto the connector.

It was all as big around as that of like a 20 oz drink bottle.

She leaned over and grabbed a small long spool like electrical wire and reached under and plugged it at a connection right there at where the hose one was. Then she reached over to the bag that had both the canteen and a like big square 6 volt battery.

Reaching down into the bag she seemed to have flipped some switch on and then a humming sound started up and the whole damn thing began to vibrate, making that long tip dance about wildly.

Looking at him and then me seeing the horrid fear of what she was about to do, she decided maybe it was best if she didn’t do this.

Explaining it something new she had Leprechaun make for her, of which He acknowledged he knew him. And she just wanted me to be the first to have the pleasure of it.

Especially since now knowing what had been found out about my secret.

So she reached over to that bag turned the vibrator switch on it off, and reached under and unplugged both hose and wires to the huge cock.

Saying your very lucky sweetie pie, that your man here stepped up for you otherwise I would used it like I wanted to.

Now having it all packed up again, she told me; Don' t you worry sweetie pie this is not my only play toy.

So she went and put the canteen and battery pack back in her cabinet, then left the room again.

I was so relieved and unafraid again, that she wasn' t going to fuck me with huge damn thing. Thanking him for having stepped in and saving me from that horrible ordeal she was wanting to put me through.

Oh I was ready to be fucked, I' ll not deny that and by her, I wanted her to fuck me I certainly did, but not with something like that at all, something like pinky as I call it, that he gave me would absolutely be fine.

He came to me as I lay there as I was, and asked me if indeed I really wanted her to fuck me? Yes I told him, but not with anything like what she had and wanted to use.

With that he leaned over and kissed me passionately, and breaking our kiss he said that was to keep me heated and ready, and that knowing her she was going to fuck me with a huge cock, he knew her all to well to know that was going to happen. And there was no telling just what she would bring in here for me next.

As we were talking I heard her back at that door unbolting it again and came back in the room that towel over her waist again and I was relieved to see that ever she had under it this time was not anywhere near the hugeness the one showed under the towel.

She had re locked the door after coming back inside the room, as she walked over I see whatever it was under that towel this time was indeed big, really big and my fears and wandering' s of it even going in me had me scared again.

Walking right back to stand there right between my legs she dropped the towel again, now this one was nowhere near that huge she had in thickness and length but it was still really big, and more so than that, It was Black!

It had a big head on it with a really long shaft as long or longer than the prior one, and it to had this little tapered tip like the last one which made it seem really odd and weird being so out of place as man' s cock replica. And it to had a hole that was very visible, As I gasped out seeing that it was in itself immense and really big.

She just stood there watching my feared awe of what she had now, and said, oh yes sweetie pie this is one I' m going to fuck you with.

That said she walked away back over to that cabinet as that huge long black thing swung and danced about from between her legs as she reached and got that same canteen and battery pack and accessories I guess is the best way to tell it.

Brought it right back over to the altar set it down where it had been before and plugged everything right back into it then back under just like the last one.

Then stood there saying it would take a moment or two to get it heated and ready for use.

I hadn' t figured any of it out as yet, just why there had to be a hose involved in all this and that huge canteen?

But she did reach over and flipped that switch and it began to vibrate just like the last one, the tip of this one wildly dancing from the vibrations.

She then told him as she reached into that canteen bag and brought out a tube a lube telling him to come and get it greased up so she could fuck me with it.

He just went and took it and rubbed the whole huge black down so it would make it much easier for me to be able to take it.

Then she made him rub my pussy lips and shove two fingers up in me and get my pussy ready, and when he did that I bucked and screamed out in pleasure then felt this really strange heated feeling on all my lips and inside my pussy where had used it.

I became absolutely on fire again as she was telling me that' s it sweetie pie get that little pussy hot and ready, let it work through you so I can fuck you senseless soon with my big black cock!

It made me absolutely gasp out and scream out in the heated fire going through my pussy, and worse than that I began to get so aroused from it all the torment of starting to want to beg and plead to be fucked took over me. I was now pleading with her to fuck me!

He had now moved around her and came back up to me leaned over and kissing me as we got fever-ant into it, I was now fully moaning and grunting out in womanly need to be fucked. As he broke our kiss and said are you ready for her to fuck you? Yes I screamed, Oh Yes fuck me, Fuck me.

She broke in and asked me if I wanted to be fucked by her big black cock, and she would not even start until I begged for it.

Yes I screamed out Oh Yes fuck me with your black cock, Oh fuck me with me with it!

He then went and sat down in his voyeur chair wanting to be right there up close and see clearly what that black cock was going to do to my pussy.

Festival

The festival was in town, and of course Emma and I had to go. We strolled around for a while nibbling on cotton candy and sneaking kisses, and then I didn’t win the teddy bear at the milk pail toss, and the guess-your-weight guy guessed my weight on the nose, 177, “because you were wearing shoes,” Emma said, although there wasn’t a scale involved—it was an honor system, and then Emma tried the milk pail toss and won a teddy bear with her first throw, though it seemed to me her baseball didn’t hit anything, but when you’re as cute as Emma good things happen.

The sky was turning a lurid pink, with lightning in the distance, but the Merry-Go-Round with two dozen silver steeds beckoned. Before mounting her stallion, Emma handed me her sandals. “Because last time I was on a carousel I lost them,” she said. Then she asked if I wasn’t going to ride. I told I couldn’t, what with holding her sandals and teddy bear, and anyway I’d rather watch her.

The lights flashed, the calliope churned, the horses went up and down, Emma went round and round, grinning and waving and blowing me kisses. She was fun to watch. Then one time as her horse galloped right at me her dress flew up and underneath I could see Emma was bare.

A revolution later the ride ended. I helped Emma off her horse. “That was so fun!” she said.

“Exciting to watch, too,” I told her. “Did you go panty-less as a preemptive measure?”

Emma’s eyes twinkled. “You had your hands full with my shoes and my teddy bear,” she said, “and anyway I prefer to ride bareback.”

The wind freshened. We could hear thunder now. “Want to know a secret?” Emma asked.

I did.

“Much as I like riding carousel horses, I’d rather ride you.”

A moment after this announcement, the rain came hard and fast. Everyone sought shelter.

Everyone but Emma. “Whee!” she said, whirling around.

“Your teddy bear is going to get soaked.”

She took the bear from my hands and handed him to a little girl riding her dad’ s shoulders toward the parking lot. Then she took my hand, and in my ear she whispered, “Ever had a Ferris Wheel fuck?”

Naughty Pussy

The cost of Joy rescuing her cat from a precarious perch was a sore back. When the ache persisted for three days, Joy made an appointment with Dr.Brad, a back specialist. The treatment, Dr.Brad determined, involved extensive massage. Dr. Brad applied his skilled hands to Joy, and soon she purred with pleasure. The pain was gone, replaced by a sense of serenity and well-being. “I feel so good,” she sighed.

“Would you like to feel even better?” Dr.Brad asked. He explained that the full cure required getting deep into Joy’ s core.

“My core?” Joy questioned. “In common parlance, your pussy,” the doctor said.

“If you think it best,” Joy said.

“I do,” the doctor declared.

He positioned Joy on the table, head down, ass up, and after stimulating her lubricious vulva with his fingers and tongue, he determined that she was wet enough for penetration. Slowly he pushed his penis into Joy’ s welcoming cunt. She moaned and opened, accepting him fully. He fucked her slowly, over the course of the next hour bringing her to half a dozen orgasms, each more powerful than the previous.

“Come in me!” she cried out, and Dr.Brad fulfilled her plea. Jet after potent jet of warm semen splashed her excited cervix. Joy came one final time, her cunt swallowing all the doctor’ s cock had to offer.

Back home that evening, Joy sat on the couch petting her naughty pussy. “If you want to climb another tree, it’s okay with me,” Joy told the creature. “But you don’t have to on my account. I’ve booked refresher treatments with Dr.Brad for the rest of your nine lives.”

Daniella Practicing

When Emma came in from working in the garden, she could hear Daniella practicing piano in the next room. It sounded good. Emma listened for a moment then went to take her shower. She made sure she wasn’t in the shower long because she wanted to hear more of Daniella playing. But when she came out, there was only silence. Still holding her towel, Emma stepped into the piano room.

What happened?” Emma asked.

“I was a bad girl,” Daniella said.

“What do you mean?”

“I was playing the Bach so badly. It was depressing. I decided to play with myself instead.”

“Play with yourself?” Emma questioned, the towel slipping to the carpet.

“Masturbating.”

“Oh,” Emma said. “Please don’t let me stop you.”

“Too embarrassing,” Daniella said.

“If you let me watch, I promise not to interfere. You won’t even notice I’m here.”

“You’ll think it’s silly,” Daniella said.

“I won’t. Why would I think it’s silly?”

“I was trying to see if I could come just from touching my nipples. I was getting pretty close to the climax.”

“Please let me watch,” Emma said. “I’ll just sit on this chair and be all but invisible.”

“Maybe you watching will be that extra turn-on I need,” Daniella said. “Maybe if you sat on the chair with your legs spread...”

Emma sat on the chair with her legs spread.

“Now put your hands behind your back, like if you were handcuffed.”

Emma put her hands behind her back. “It’s a little uncomfortable,” she said.

“Okay, now grip the chair. And hold still.”

Emma gripped the chair.

Daniella brought a hand to her breast. Her fingers caressed and pinched the nipple.

“Your nipples are so sexy,” Emma said.

“Shut up,” Daniella said. “You promised not to interfere. That would be cheating.”

“Sorry,” Emma said.

Daniella resumed stimulation of her nipple.

“Does this excite you?” she asked Emma. “Watching me touch my breast?”

“It makes me wet,” Emma said.

“Hush, you aren’t supposed to talk. Just watch. But maybe I can make good use of your wetness. Would that be okay?”

Emma nodded.

Daniella moved closer to Emma’s chair. Her hand went to Emma’s sex. “Oh, you are wet,” she said. Her fingers coated with Emma’s moisture, she resumed touching her nipple, the slippery fingers circling and circling.

“I can’t,” Daniella moaned. “I’m almost there, and then it goes away. Maybe I should go back to the Bach."

"No," Emma said. "Maybe if you lie down on the piano bench."

Daniella pulled the piano bench away from the piano and lay down on her back.

"Now touch your nipple," Emma said. "That's right. That's right. You're getting there. You're getting there."

Daniella touched and mewled, but she could quite reach orgasm.

"Oh, sweetie," Emma whispered. "Your pussy looks so sweet. There's a pearl of love juice in your fuck hole. Oh, darling, I have to taste it."

Without waiting for permission, Emma knelt between Daniella's legs and fastened her lips to Daniella's clit.

With a gush, Daniella came.

Emma kept kissing and licking and tonguing, and Daniella kept coming.

At last she let Daniella relax.

"That was so nice," Emma told her lover. "Better than Bach?"

Daniella sighed, a clear yes of a sigh.

"And it was okay that I interfered?"

Another yes of a sigh.

"Great," Emma said. "Tomorrow we're going to do Rachmaninoff."

Celine’s Christmas

I wake to Celine sucking my cock. Celine’ s blowjobs are beyond compare. She knows all the tricks, naughty and nice, so that I soon go crazy wanting to come in her mouth and wanting the blowjob to go on forever.

“Oh, sweetie, you’ re awake,” she says, giving me a moment’ s breather before resuming her licks and sucks. She grins big. “Merry Christmas honey.” Her tongue twirls and swirls. Her lips kiss and hum. Her fingers stroke and twist and toy and tantalize.

“But Christmas doesn’ t come for um um almost nine monts,” I manage to mumble.

Celine chuckles even with my cock caressing the back of her throat. “Preparation,” she says, and I have to wonder in both delight and apprehension if this blowjob might go on for days. Her mouth wraps my cock in a succession of succulent sucks. She draws me in with her mouth and her eyes. She takes me closer and closer to the point of no return.

“I need to...” I moan, “ ... come.”

“I know you do,” Celine replies, having abruptly stopped. “By the way, in case you’ re interested, I’ ve thought of what I want for Christmas.”

“Yes, yes, anything,” I blurt.

She smiles a naughty smile. “A piano.”

“Yes, yes, a piano,” I agree. My head knows there isn’ t room for a piano in our tiny apartment. My cock just wants more of her mouth.

“And a house to put it in,” Celine says, smiling an even naughtier smile.

“Yes, yes, a house.”

Celine nods thoughtfully, and then she smiles the naughtiest smile. “And kids to play in the yard and take piano lessons.”

“Yes, yes, piano lessons,” I say before what she’s said sinks in.

“Starting now,” she says, mounting me with exquisite grace.

Between the two of us we make everything come true.

www.ingramcontent.com/pod-product-compliance
Lightning Source LLC
LaVergne TN
LVHW080819170826
845678LV00011B/2077
* 9 7 9 8 8 4 6 7 6 7 3 6 2 *